I0736499

TUAN NGO

Perpetual Love

WORKBOOK PRESS LLC
187 E Warm Springs Rd,
Suite B285, Las Vegas, NV 89119, USA

Website: https://workbookpress.com/
Hotline: 1-888-818-4856
Email: admin@workbookpress.com

Ordering Information:
Quantity sales. Special discounts are available on quantity purchases by corporations, associations, and others.
For details, contact the publisher at the address above.

ISBN-13:   978-1-952754-57-9 (Paperback Version)
              978-1-952754-58-6 (Digital Version)

REV. DATE: 22/07/2020

Contents

Dedication

In loving memory of my parents, Cu Ngo and Phuong Nguyen, who had helped me to get an education during my formative years.

To my brothers and sisters, for their sharing with me happy times, as well as, difficult ones, under the same roof.

My wife, Lilian, for her self-sacrifice in rearing and tending the children.

My two children, Michael and Vivian, for their patience, during my absence From the family foyer.

To the grandeur, majesty, generosity of the United States of America.

June 03rd, 2020.

Preface

Notice that in many newspapers, magazines, and books publishing daily, there is not one column reserved for poems or literature. And notice that in the age of the Internet, many people, especially the young generation, are totally absorbed in front of the computers with video games, texting, forgetting about humanity.

Therefore, after many years of composing poems, writing short stories, I have decided to publish it for the general public. Hopefully, this book, consisting of many short, romantic poems, will sound an echo in the vast emptiness of the humdrums of life. All the romances described here are fictional. Any resemblance with real life is beyond the intention of the author.

Thank you very much for the help of all the editorial and management staff of Xlibris publishing house, without which this book would not be published today.

Tuan Ngo
Fall 2012

Love Me Forever

Yesterday, I visited you at your home.
It snowed heavily, and the east wind was bitterly cold.
You looked at me, and your eyes were in tears.
Holding my hands in yours, you told me,
"Love me forever."
Oh my god! It is very difficult to find fidelity in love
Nowadays.
But please do not worry, my dear.
I will promise you one thing for sure:
"The snow and the rain are my road companions.
I will follow you, in the four corners of the world.
As long as the earth still turns around the sun
And my heart still ticks,
Then my love with you still sticks."

••••• *Enchanted Mekong River* •••••

The Mekong River flows downstream.
The boat is floating aimlessly in the waters.
Suddenly, I heard a song sung by a ferryboat lady.
My heart is fluttering and racing.
Outside the boat, I heard the sound of the
Lapping small waves striking the wood.
Inside the boat, I feel giddy.
Is it due to the effects of the drink,
The motion sickness, or my fluttering heart?

●···· The Second-Place Lady ····●

Dear Mother-in-Law,
Do not be sad if your son loves me.
I know from the depth of my heart
That he belongs to you.
He might love me during his youth,
But for you only, his love is lasting forever.

You gave birth to him.
Your shadow was framed into his heart.
Although I was loved by him as such,
I always occupy a second place after you
In his heart.

Dear Mother-in-Law,
Do not be jealous during some mornings
Or some nights your son might miss me
More than you.
But to him I was always compared to a
Light wind. You are always the harbor of
His love.

A breeze, such am I.
Other women might steal his heart from me.
But I know from the depth of my heart that
A smoldering fire is always lit up in his heart
For you.

He might share his love with me for all his remaining life,
Or he might leave me for someone else tomorrow.
But I know for sure one thing: that you are always
On his mind.
So whatsoever happens,
I always occupy the second place after you in
His heart.
By second-place person

Translated into English by Tuan Ngo, MD
From a poem by HP Los Angeles, California, USA
1340 Pacific time

Melancholy

If you did not flirt with me,
We would not have been in love with
Each other.
Then, there would not have been a painful sequel
Between us.
And we would not have ended up in tears and sorrows.

I have already swallowed the bitter pill of love.
Now, I need to get rid of the intricacy of my love affair
Off my mind
So that my baggage of romance becomes lighter, smaller,
And easy to carry on.
And from now on, the music of serenade would be
Turned off for long.

And now, you are out of my sight,
But still not out of my mind.
I feel melancholy.
I regret the old romantic days.
The day when, clad in loosely fit pajamas,
I looked out of the balcony,
Seeing the rain falling down,
Smelling the scent of jasmine flowers below,
In the garden, listening to the chirping of
The birds, and hearing the sound of the
Whistling wind blowing by the trees.
Those days are gone.

If you did not flirt with me,
I would not have melancholy.

By Duong Thuy Ngo
12:55 PM
03-17-2013

●····· The Ties of Affection ·····●

Prologue

This poem is fiction. Any resemblance with reality is coincidental. One girl forced into marriage's bondage overseas sent back a letter to her mother at home through this poem.

Mom, please do not marry me to a faraway land.
I can take care of you when you will become
Old and frail.
Once, there was a young girl living in a countryside,
Who loved a young man in her hometown.
But one day, a matchmaker coaxed her to marry a stranger
In a faraway land, overseas.
Over there, the girl sent a letter to her mom at home.
My body is not chattel for sale.
Please do not steal my childhood.
And please, do not rob me of my innocence.
Il ne faut pas voler mon enfance.
Et s'il vous plait, ne volez pas mon innocence.
"Who split the moon into two halves?
Half of it is here, and the other half
Is a thousand miles away."
Mom, please do not marry me off in
A faraway land.
I could take care of you
When you grow old and frail.

Without Her

Prologue

Because you told me how important you are in the poem "Without Him," let me tell you the other side of my story in this poem, "Without Her," to be fair. Lovingly yours,

She

Without her, who wakes you up early in the morning for you
To commute to work?
Who prepares healthy food and clean water for you to
Eat and drink at dinner?
Without her, who pays the bills of the mortgage, cars,
Utilities, insurances, etc?
Who prunes the trees, mows the lawns, and plants the
Flowers in the garden?
Who cleans and sweeps the house, in and out?
Who sits next to you and listens to your love stories?

Without her, who laughs when you laugh, and
Who cries when you cry?
And who else but her shares your sorrows and tears?
Who else but her gives you great moments in life?
And who gave birth to our beautiful children?
And . . .
When you go to war, far away from home, in
Afghanistan, in Helmand Province, or Khyber Pass,
At home, it is she who tills and plows the rice paddies.
And your elderly, sick mother will be well cared by her.
When the war is over, the country is in peace.
You will return home.

Here is she, still waiting for you, faithful and alone.
Her allure is brisk. Her eyes are sparkling with joy.
Her smile is broader than ever.
And lo and behold,
Wave after wave of heavy stalks of
Blond, ripe grains of rice in vast rice paddies,
Stretched to the horizon, are undulating melodiously
Under the wind and waiting for you to harvest.
With loving thoughts and ever yours,
She.

Composed by
Tuan Ngo, MD
September 19, 2012,
2117 Pacific time
Los Angeles, California, USA
The End

Without Her

Prologue

Because you told me how important you are in the poem "Without Him," let me tell you the other side of my story in this poem, "Without Her," to be fair.

Lovingly yours,
She

Without her,
Who wakes you up early in the morning for you to
Commute to work?
Who prepares healthy food and clean water for you
To eat and drink at dinner?
Without her, who pays the mortgage, car, utilities,
And health insurance bills?
Who prunes the trees, mows the lawns, and plants the
Flowers in the garden?
Who cleans and sweeps the house, in and out?
Who sits next to you and listens to your tale of
Love stories?

Without her,
Who laughs when you laugh, and who
Cries and you cry?
And who else but she shares your sorrows and tears?
Who else but she gives you great moments in life?
And who gave birth to our beautiful children?
And . . .

When you go to war, far away from home, in

Afghanistan, Helmand Province, Khyber Pass,
Or in Iraq, Basra, Ramadi, Baghdad,
At home, it is she who tills and plows the rice paddies.
And it is she who cares for your elderly, sick mother,
As well as the cattle and your pet dog, named Candy.
And . . .

When the war is over, the country is in peace.
You will return home. Farewell to arms.
There she will be, still waiting for you,
Faithful and alone.
Her allure is brisk.
Her eyes sparkle with joy.
Her smile is broader than ever.
And . . .

Lo and behold,
Wave after wave of heavy stalks of blond,
Ripe grains of rice, in vast rice paddies,
Stretched to the horizon, undulate melodiously
Under the breeze and
Waiting for you to harvest. W

ith loving thoughts and ever yours,
She.

Composed by
Duong Thuy Ngo
April 7, 2013, 10:25 AM
Pacific time. The end.

●···· My Sweetheart ····●

This is the English version of the poem "My Sweetheart."
This is fiction. Any resemblance with reality is coincidental.

Poem
My Sweetheart

1. Yesterday, I passed by my sweetheart's home.
2. On her doorstep were littered the red petals of flowers
3. And the blown-up bodies of the red firecrackers.
4. An emotion suddenly gripped my heart.
5. I brisked up my pace and felt numb and sad.

6. Back home, I opened a thick book in which
7. I kept the compressed petals of the flower
8. Many years ago.
9. The color of the petals is still the same.
10. It is not fading away.
11. Oh my god! My love was crossed by
12. My darling.
13. All my love and hope were gone down the
14. Drain to the river by her unfaithfulness.

Composed by Tuan Ngo, MD
June 30, 2013
14: PM Pacific time

Lovable

In seeing you, I feel in eagerness.
You speak the same language like
In our native country.
At dinner, your meal consists of
Soup with bitter vegetable and a
Dish of bamboo shoots dipped in
Brine, cooked by low fire.
I am happy because I am not got
Strayed in the strange land.
For many years, although you lived
From hand to mouth daily, but
You have not forgotten the old,
Direct, Southern greeting style.
"Eat the French cake that I made.
Do you think that I could open
The bakery business in the future?
Seeing you gives me a flashback of
The coconut trees,
Of the freshwater rivers of the
Mekong Delta
And of the sampans floating slowly
Along them.

By Duong Thuy Ngo
April 7, 2013,
9:10 PM Pacific time

•····· Autumn's Overture ·····•

My sweet, did the fall begin yet?
Hanging, foggy curtains of mist blocked my view
At every corner around here.
Nature has changed its coat's color into
A red and yellow one.
Suddenly, I felt sadness.

My sweet, did the fall begin yet?
It seemed to me that you were very
Attached to me at the good-bye time.
Your shoulders were wet with tears.
You cried for a short and wilted love affair.

My sweet, did the fall begin yet?
I remembered your first and passionate kiss.
The love boat had a rough ride in a
Stormy sea of love passions.
It narrowly sank to the bottom of the sea.

My sweet, did the fall begin yet?
Please, do not sob heavily.
Tomorrow, the dark clouds would be
Dissipated away.
The sky would be clear.
We would walk on the same
path And we would look into the same direction.

By Tuan Ngo, MD

"La neige et le vent sont mes compagnons de route.
Tant que la terre tourne en rond autour d'elle-même
Et autour du soleil,
Et que mon Coeur bat encore,
Alors mon amour avec toi reste encore."
French translation of the last three sentences of the
English poem "Love Me Forever."

●····· *A Poem for My Mother* ·····●

There are seven wonders of the world.
But my mother is truly the eighth one.
Outside, the snowstorm blankets the sky,
But inside this house, the flame of my mother's heart
Continues to burn eternally,
And it lights me up.

By Tuan Ngo, MD
On the occasion of Mother's Day 2011

Thank You and Good-Bye to You, Dear Ex-husband

Dear ex, we are now separated!
Thank you for your past affections.
Thank you for your ardent passions of love,
Your hanging around me at noon
On the hammock, in the veranda
During the hot, sweltering summer.
Thank you for sharing our conjugal
Love for many years,
But now, you leave me for another woman!
Our love does not last long.
It is fast like the fleeting clouds in the sky,
Like the soap's bubbles, which are
Quickly forming and merging together,
And then they are bursting.
Now, you change to a different path
To form a new love affair.
Our old love liaison is now broken,
Irreconcilable.
Dear ex, if we ever meet again,
Your old flame were turned off
And were no longer yours,
Why should I regret? Why should I cry?
There is nothing left to be regretful.
Good-bye to you, the one who betrayed
My unrequited love and left in me a deep
Broken heart, which will take a long time
To heal. The end.
Broken heart.
Composed by Weeping Willow

A.k.a. HK, HK
May 24, 2010, 2120
California, USA

Self-Reflection

If I knew you, I would have told you about my
Lovely country this evening.
Please do not confuse me with Thai, Japanese, or
Korean people.
I am very much different from them.
Vietnam's geographical shape looks like a letter S.
This land is very poor and narrow.
But the people who live there are generous.
They love other people, are easygoing, and have
An open heart.
Unfortunately, this country has suffered a lot of misfortunes.
For thirty years continuously, there have been wars and destruction.
Fires and burns, blood loss, and millions of lost lives unaccounted for.
Therefore, sometimes you see me drooping down my head.
It is because of my reflection, gnawing at my conscience.

By Tuan Ngo, MD
April 29, 2013, 2125 Pacific time

●····· The Confessions ·····●

Prologue

This poem, "The Confessions," will be published here in three parts. This is the English translation of the poem "Loi thu toi." A few lines in the context have been changed by me. The author here, D. T. Ngo, is the translator.

Part I. The Confessions

I am a citizen of the United States of America.
I just survived a big turmoil of history.
I dyed my hair to make me look younger.
And I changed my name for easy spelling.

Yes, I was a small, malnourished guy named Tee.
I was digging potatoes in the new economic zone.
I was living in a dark hut house at night with no electricity, no plumbing system
near a river named Small.
At dinner, scanty rice soup filled my stomach instead of
Cooked rice.

Now, I forget it all. I am an ungrateful man.
My rotten bones will be laid to rest upon death in
A foreign land.
During my sleep, I dream of a Bahamas vacation and
Las Vegas.
And I dream of living one day in the
White House.
(to be continued . . .)

Composed by Duong Thuy Ngo
June 9, 2013
1340 Pacific time

The Confessions
(Part 2) English Version

I stand up still to salute the flag at each football game.
But I hate to do this at other ceremonies, national flag
Raising.
Who died? Who were in jails?
Who cares about that?
It is not my business to shoulder the burdens of
My native land.

I prefer, rather, to talk about real estate and
Stock markets than vegetables, rice, potatoes, and
Counting maniocs.
That is life. There are days up and down.
I talk about my painful, not pleasant past.

I like to show off mansions and big houses,
And luxury, convertible, exotic sport cars.
I want to hide the other family debts that
I still owe, unpaid.
The debt of my father's love with his still-
Open eyes upon his death, in distress.
The debt of the blood flowing in my veins
From my old mother.

I forget that I had millions of other displaced
Children, roaming and wandering all over
The country during the horrible times of war.
I was one among them.
I was born malnourished, underweight, on those days and nourished from a
trickle of
Breast milk in the skinny arms of my mother.

By Duong Thuy Ngo, MD
June 9, 2013
2140 Pacific time

The Confessions

(Part 3) English Version. The End.

I forget that I had millions of other brothers
Who were jailed in camps, jungles, mountains,
And they died without graves, tombstones, no names, like animals.

I forget that I had thousands of my sisters,
Lost and unfound in Thailand and Cambodia.
I do not know that at night they did dream of
Their mothers' land, near the row of coconut
Trees and the rice paddies.

In June gloom, with heavy rains,
I heard of someone's cry from across
The Pacific Ocean
"Tee boy, you are a betrayer."
I woke up and I realized, it was me.

Composed by Duong Thuy Ngo, MD
June 9, 2013
2200 Pacific time
The end

•···· *Paradise Lost* ····•

Part 1

Pardon me, my dear, beloved wife.
You have suffered a life of negligence.
While strolling in the orchard of papaya trees,
I overheard your conversation with your mother,
Through a cell phone, next to a papaya tree, the following:
"When he becomes the general director of this
Big company, our lives will become better."

Pardon me, my faithful, virtuous wife;
Innumerable nights, you spent alone,
Under unshared blankets and single wet-with-tears
Pillows.
While I was still chasing after business deals in
A global, competitive world, you still hoped to find
"a light at the end of a tunnel."
He said, "When he becomes a global director, my
Children will see the face of their father at home."

Paradise Lost
Part 2

But one day, you heard a rumor that I had
A love affair with a young mistress.
You were startled and thought that I had a
Second "outpost."
When you confronted me, I told you that
This was only a lie.
Suddenly your lips turned blue and your
Whole body was shaking.
I thought that you had a heart attack.

"When he becomes a tycoon, he will go for vacation
With me to relax, every year."

Part 3

Pardon me, my trustful, unwavering wife.
I sacrificed you and the lives of our children
In my pursuit of personal fame and fortune.
I have sacrificed you, as a pawn, in seeking
For mirage and delusions of grandeur and gold.
After many years of neglect, our children's path

Turned the wrong way.
All your lives have been bet and lost totally in this
Gamble of happiness in life partnership with me.

All your expected vacations and full-time companionship
Never bore fruit.
Under a dim light of a small, slender, unique
Wax candle, lit up on a small table all night, with your
Head drooping
All your confidence and hope in me are
Totally vanished.
And your beautiful dream, sharing with me,
Has been betrayed and wholly shattered into
Thousand small pieces, beyond repair.
Alleluia! A paradise lost!

By Tuan Ngo, MD
September 30, 2012
12:15 PM Pacific time
Los Angeles, California, USA

The Dinner

Mom, I am very much hungry!
Son, please go to the kitchen and
Carry the rice pot out.
Mom is busy slicing the eggplants on
The plate.
But, my son, please wait a moment till your
Daddy comes home.
Outside of the house, the bright and full moon
Shines over the still countryside.
As dusk settles in, the dark sky is lit up
All over by myriad of sparkling little stars like
Thousands of glittering diamonds.
Now, my dad leads the buffalo back home.
He is in. He rests and he relaxes himself by
Smoking tobacco leaves through a cylindrical
Water pipe, made in bamboo.
And Mom puts away the harrow. And
She scrapes out the balls of rice wrapped in
The sheath of the leaves of the acacia tree,
Left over since this morning breakfast.
And then, gathered around the fireplace in
The kitchen, the whole family sits down and
Eats happily the frugal dinner, which consists of
Steamed-rice, hot soup, eggplants,
And salted vegetables.

Translated from the poem
"Bua com chieu" by Dr. Tuan Ngo.
October 29, 2011
Los Angeles, California, USA
9:42 PM Pacific time

My Sweet, Is There Any News in California?

My sweet, is there any news in California?
Yes, in California, there are many wide freeways
Running up north and down south.
Its nickname is Golden State, where
There was a Gold Rush.
Its state flower is California poppy.
Its bird is a quail.

My sweet, is there any news in California?
Here is San Francisco City with its suspension
Bridge crossing through the sea.
And there is Stanford University with
Its large campus and hills and mountains.
Here is San Jose City, Mountain View, Cupertino,
Palo Alto, called Silicon, Internet Valley.

My sweet, is there any news in California?
There is Napa Valley with its famous wine
And vineyards.
Here is Los Angeles City, and
There is Chinatown.
Here is Hollywood City with its movie industry
And its famous actors and actresses, Oscar's awards.
Here is Disneyland, called the Happiest Place on Earth,
Where people, from all over the world, come
To be entertained, in Anaheim.
Here is Westminster City with its Little Saigon town.

My sweet, is there any news in California?

In California there is sun, sand, sea, and surf.
The leaves of the trees are evergreen.

There are many long beaches with white sand
Stretched from Pelican Beach to San Diego Bay.
Here are Huntington, Malibu, Laguna, Newport,
Monterey, just to name a few.
I will give you a ride to all the cities and streets
In California, with the aid of Mapquest, Tomtom,
Magellan's guidance.

My sweet, is there any news in California?
Holding your hands in my hands, we walk
Barefoot along the beaches at sunset.
And I will count the sparkling stars at night
On the celestial ceiling above.
Strong waves, coming offshore, pound
On the seashores.
But deep in my heart, I feel inundated by
A rising tide of love's passions.

Composed by Tuan Ngo, MD
October 4, 2012
08:40 PM Pacific time
Los Angeles, California, USA

Without Me

Without me, who accompanied you in the day of snowstorm?
Who dated you at the end of school hours?
Who held your hands by telling you tales of love stories?

Without me, who gave you the first kiss passionately in life?
Who played the guitar while you were singing love songs?
Who guided your first, awkward, small steps on the ballroom
Dancing floor?
Without me, who sat next to you in a Starbucks coffeehouse in
A gloomy day of heavy rain?

And without me, who will scratch your back at the
Sunset of your life?

Composed by Duong Thuy Ngo
September 4, 2011

Author Biography

1950. Born in Hanoi, Vietnam.

1954. Moved to Saigon, South Vietnam.

1968. Graduated French baccalauréat high school diploma, at Lasalle Taberd High School, Saigon, Vietnam.

1969–1978. Studied at Saigon Medical School.

1978. Graduated a medical doctor.

1981. Arrived to the United States of America.

Now, medical doctor, nephrologist, working in Los Angeles, California, at Feinstein & Roe, MD, Inc.
Married and has two children: one boy, one girl.
Likes to write books and poems and draw.

About the Book

This book is about selected lyrical poems. It depicts loyalty in love, fidelity, love between man and woman; in family, between children toward their parents, filial duty; under the view angle of Far East Asia and about the inequality of love for the woman, under the Far Eastern view angle; and in some parts of the world, romantic love.

Copyedited by Joy Thangmuanching Manlun
Reviewed by Kimberly Joyce Veloso

1 This discovery is from Copernicus, a Dutch astronomer.

2 Mekong is the name of a long river originating from Tibet, flowing through China, Laos, Thailand, Cambodia, and Vietnam.

3 The phrase in quotation marks is from a famous poet, Du Nguyen, in the Kieu story.

4 French translation of two lines immediately above.

5 Thirty years: from 1945 until April 30, 1975.

6 Outpost meaning "another mistress" (metaphor by author). 7 Mapquest: Software to find location on the map from AOL. Tomtom and Magellan are trademarks name of their devices to pinpoint location on the street map.